STEPPING *into the*
RING

STEPPING *into the*
RING

Fighting for Hope over Despair
IN THE BATTLE AGAINST BREAST CANCER

Nicole Johnson

W PUBLISHING GROUP™

www.wpublishinggroup.com

A Division of Thomas Nelson, Inc.
www.ThomasNelson.com

Published by W Publishing Group, a Division of Thomas Nelson, Inc.,
P.O. Box 141000, Nashville, Tennessee 37214.

Library of Congress Cataloging-in-Publication Data

Johnson, Nicole.
Stepping into the ring: fighting for hope over despair
in the battle against breast cancer/by Nicole Johnson.

p. cm.

ISBN 0-8499-1781-6

1. Breast cancer--Patients--Religious life.
2. Breast Cancer--Religious aspects--Christianity. I. Title.

BV4910.33 .J64 2003
248.8'619699449--dc21
2002010583

Printed in the United States of America
02 03 04 05 06 07 PHX 7 6 5 4 3 2 1

Contents

Every three minutes a woman in this country is diagnosed with breast cancer. Although I haven't had the disease myself, I have been deeply inspired by courageous women who have. Some of these women have shared their stories with me, in the hope that I will offer encouragement to those who follow them, and support to those walking alongside them. I have written the pages that follow for them, and on their behalf.

ROUND I

The Heavyweight Champion of the World

"I just came in because I found a little knot . . ."

"The doctor will see you now . . ."

"It won't aspirate; we'll have to do a biopsy . . ."

It was all perfectly routine. There really wasn't anything to worry about. Every day more women go through this than buy handbags at department stores. I was determined not to borrow trouble. I wasn't going to let fear get the upper hand. I didn't even tell anyone that I was going in. I'd all but forgotten about it until the next morning.

I was standing in the kitchen when the phone rang, and I knew. Not with a half knowing, but with a jolt that seized me so hard liquid spilled out of my eyes before I said hello. I listened to her voice asking me

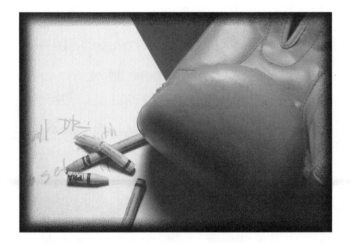

to come back, and I wrote something down with a crayon that was lying on the counter. I smelled leftover bacon from breakfast.

"Thank you for calling." I lied through my teeth as I broke the crayon in half, and then I completely lost track of everything. I guess I fainted—I don't know what happened. But the next thing I knew they were all standing over me—my daughter, my son, my husband, my neighbor . . . and a paramedic.

"Mom?" "Mommy?" "Honey?" "Kathy?" "Lady?" I thought I was dead. Actually, I thought I might as well be. Breast cancer?

"I'm fine," I said, lying for the second time that day. I felt stupid as I got up. Now what was I going to say? No one knew about the call I had just gotten. No one knew I had even gone to the doctor. I literally wished I were bleeding so there would be something to show what was going on inside me.

Later, I was able to find the words to tell my husband. I was strong until he cried. But nothing could prepare me for having to find the right words to fill the questioning pools in the eyes of my five-year-old daughter. My son was a little easier, if only because this disease could never touch him in the same way. More tears than all the water I ever drank in my life flowed out of me. None of us knew what this meant, except terrible loss no matter how it played out. I wasn't sure which scared me more: dying, or living without my breast.

Finding out I had cancer was like going to sleep in my own bed and suddenly waking up in the middle of a boxing ring. Out of the clear blue I am standing toe-to-toe with the Heavyweight Champion of the

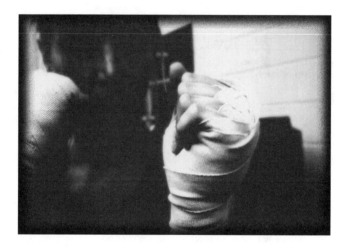

World, the crowd is looking on, and I am in my pajamas and don't even know how to throw a punch.

"Your chance of survival is much greater if we remove it totally . . ."

"I'd like to schedule the surgery soon . . ."

"You should consider reconstruction immediately . . ."

Every line was a physical punch. Blow after blow the words kept coming, until I was sick to my stomach and dizzy with fatigue. The wind was knocked out of me and I couldn't breathe. I couldn't say anything, my tongue was numb, and my eyes refused to blink.

"How does next Tuesday look?"

"Honey, schedule the surgery; I'll cancel the trip."

"Mommy, are you going to be okay?"

Inside I was screaming, *NO!!! Please, God, no.* But outside, my mouth still wasn't working and my head wouldn't even cooperate by moving from one side to the other.

Everything in me wanted to go back to the moment in time before I got the report, but that was simply not an option. I was already in the ring. The only choice was whether or not to go forward. I could keep standing there, literally getting killed, or I could begin to fight back.

ROUND II

Putting on the Gloves

At first I was angry. I mean *angry*. People don't like you to be angry, but it's totally appropriate. Cancer is not normal; it is a group of cells gone terribly wrong. Perhaps when death takes a person who is old and suffering it is a kind of tender mercy, but when it takes the young, when it leaves children without a mother, it is a cruel thief and it deserves our outrage and anger.

Cancer is a terrorist. That dawned on me on September 11, 2001. I sat in front of the TV with my family and the rest of the nation watching the Twin Towers fall and crying my eyes out. But hours into it, I knew a lot of my tears were coming from a deeper place inside. I was angry for New York, and I was angry for myself. Cancer is a foreign invader that unexpectedly attacks and cruelly changes the landscape of a woman's body. New York is still New York, but it has been changed forever. And so have I. And while we can take swift justice against the damage that has been done, we cannot replace what has been lost. We survive, but we are left with the loss and the ache in the rubble left behind.

On the inside I'm all I ever was—but hello, we live in a world where the outside matters. And my breasts mattered to me. I've never had great ones, but I had them. They seemed to please my husband; they fed my babies, and they definitely made my stomach look smaller. When you pledge allegiance you put your hand over your heart, but it's really your breast. When you cross your heart and hope to die, it's right in between your breasts that you make that promise. I didn't want to live without them—either one of them. No, that's

not true. I didn't want to *have* to live without them. But I also didn't want to die in order to keep them. This is not a hard choice intellectually, but when were breasts intellectual?

I wore myself out swinging at this elusive terrorist. I tried to bob and weave and punch and punch and punch. But it was like going toe-to-toe with the Stay Puff Marshmallow Man. My frustration and anger grew because there was nothing to hit. So I'd spar with my mother or my husband—taking my cancer anger out on them.

My mother was letting the kids do something I didn't like and I said to her, "Why don't you wait to do that until I'm gone?" I knew it was an awful thing to say. It's so easy to hurt others when you're hurting. Then I just broke down and sobbed and let her hold me for a while.

One day out of the clear blue I threw a jab at my husband. "You know you say you'll still love me without my breast, but you won't have much choice, will you?" He stopped what he was doing, looked at me and said, "If I lost my arm, would you love me any less?" I said, "Of course not." Then he took my face in his hands, and he said, "Can you trust me to love as well as you?"

Oh, God, forgive me. I'm just not myself.

ROUND III

Choosing Your Corner

Women have always had a unique fellowship of suffering. A woman can walk up to another woman on the street, a complete stranger, and ask her for a tampon. And this new friend will immediately start digging around in her purse just to try to help you. But asking for a favor and finding a soul who can meet you in the middle of your pain are two different things. And when you have cancer you quickly learn the difference. It matters terribly who's in your corner.

There are plenty of well-meaning people who want to help you, but you have to be careful. Many just want to help by minimizing your loss—they'll say things like, "It's only hair," or "It's just a breast." They have no idea. Honestly, it's only hair as long as it's someone else's.

The next person who tries to tell you it's only hair, ask her about the last time she lost all hers in clumps on the floor. Or the time she had to wear a wig, which happens to be as easy as training a small rodent to sit still on your head. The truth is that people who want to minimize your pain sometimes just want to minimize theirs.

Often, the people you think will walk alongside you through cancer can't find the time to return your call. And surprisingly, the ones you never would have guessed drop everything and won't leave your side. Many well-intentioned friends don't have a clue how to enter your suffering. Let's face it, there's no handbook. No one has yet written *Suffering for Dummies* (thank God). So while they don't mean to, some friends might treat your illness with a casual word that falls ridiculously and painfully short of helping. Bless their hearts, they just

don't know. Somehow, suffering buys you membership into an exclusive club you never wanted to join. But it doesn't take long to tell who's *in* and who's *not in.*

The people who are *not in* glibly say things like, "Life will go on." What a horrible thing to say! Of course life will go on. It will go on with or without you. That's one thing that is so maddening. The world was going on when a twelve-year-old opened fire on his classmates. The world was going on when two children lost their father in a car accident. And the world was definitely going on when I got the worst news of my life. Why couldn't everything just stop? Why doesn't time stand still for each of us to acknowledge our tragedies? Other mothers were still driving their kids to school and making plans for the weekend, and deciding whether to put the lamp there or there. *STOP!* I wanted to scream at the top of my lungs. *Please stop, just for a minute.*

Yes, you know life goes on, but you're not so sure you want it to. Because whatever happens from here on, life will never be the same.

ROUND IV

Below the Belt

There are rounds in this fight when you are just hanging on for the bell. You're praying that one more punch doesn't land in your gut before that three minutes is up. Chemo is like that. I was hanging on the ropes, taking punches, trying to throw punches. My mind strained to understand all the medical information the doctor was explaining so rationally, until I was dizzy. *Come on, bell.* I would go home and look in the face of my daughter, and the tears from my heart could overflow rivers. *Please ring, bell.* But while the mind is thinking and the heart is weeping, the body still has to fight. And fight and fight, until there's no more fight left. Yes, I know. We are more than our bodies, the battle is also fought in our minds and in our spirits. But when it comes to pain, you're trapped in your body, and it's awful.

In the throes of physical pain and sickness, I just wanted to quit—mind, heart, and body. Check out, give in—crawl into a box and wait for my death. I wanted to pull the covers over my head and submit my letter of resignation to Life. I decided I would send it, "To whom it may concern, and to a few it would not concern at all."

Dear Life—

You cheated. It's not fair. This was not supposed to happen. I did not sign up for this, and no one put my name down for cancer while I wasn't looking. You have taken my life—a life that was finally going quite well—and you have wrecked it.

You have hit me before, but nothing like this. Out of the clear blue, whammo! Cancer. That blow was way below the belt. More specifically, it was a blow right in the breast, and I'm not playing anymore. You win. Are you happy now?

I will miss the sunsets and the laughter of my children, walks with my husband and the taste of homemade bread, but other than that you can have everything else. I'm too tired to fight anymore. Please accept my letter of resignation. I will be cleaning out my desk shortly. I would like to go home now.

Yours, not so truly,
Me

ROUND V

Taking It on the Chin

The ring is a frightening and lonely place. Even with the best people in your corner, you still have to be out there alone. Even with the crowd cheering for you, you're the one whose arms are aching. There is no one to fight this battle for you. Sometimes in the middle of a crowded room, I've wanted to yell out, "Does anyone here have breast cancer?" I've searched for eyes I could look into and find comfort, knowing I wasn't the only one in the fight. I don't even want to go to the bathroom alone; I certainly didn't want to go through cancer alone.

It's in the center of the ring that you face the biggest questions. Or they face you. Why me? Percentages? Too many birth-control pills? There is no answer with any real authority. My doctor tried, fumbling with facts

about genetics and childbearing, but all his medical reasoning couldn't come close to answering the deeper question of my soul. Why did the big bully of cancer choose to pick on me?

I never meant to blame God, but I did. Almost everyone does. Even people who don't have faith in God shake their fist at the sky in anger when tragedy strikes. It's just too unsatisfying to have no one to hold accountable for the unfairness of it all. We bring the question of responsibility to the doorstep of the Almighty, even if we're not sure he's even there. And if there is a God, isn't he supposed to be looking after me? Couldn't he have shielded me from this? In my confusion and pain I was afraid to get mad at God, and too mad at him not to.

It was Tuesday and I was driving the carpool,

but in my mind I was running around the ring with God. I was in the middle of all my questions, one step away from giving God an earful. Silently the tears rolled down my cheeks, the weight of my burden squeezing them out. I dropped off the kids, relieved once again that they're kids and that they don't notice when I cry. I sat in my car in the parking lot of a coffee place, feeling utterly alone. I felt like God was so far away. When something happens while someone you love is out of town, you think, *If only you'd been here* . . . So I had to tell God what happened. Not because he'd really been gone, but because I had.

So I said the hardest words out loud, "I've got cancer." There was quiet for a moment. Then it was like I heard him say softly, "I know. I know, and I'm here." And I think I heard God cry.

I was silent and still. I didn't want to figure it out anymore or try to demand an explanation. I just put my head on God's chest and wept. And wept. Somehow, in my car, his strong arms held me as I cried. I felt like Job. Here was a suffering soul who sought God's answer and, instead, got God. Not what he was expecting, and far better than what he'd asked for. "Though I walk through the valley of the shadow of death, I will fear no evil, for you are with me." There's a reason that people all around the world know Psalm 23 by heart — they've had to.

ROUND VI

Hits from the Blind Side

Just about the time I started to get my second wind a couple of glancing blows caught me totally off guard. They came on my blind side, from the direction of my corner. I wasn't prepared for the friends and well-wishers who crowded around with their clichés and cheery comfort. "Look on the bright side." "You have this disease for a reason." "God must have a wonderful purpose for allowing you to go through this." I don't like saccharine with my coffee; I like it even less with my cancer.

There is nothing like fighting for your life through unspeakable suffering to break you of bumper-sticker thinking. It used to be that a bumper sticker was a little reminder to think more deeply about something.

Now bumper stickers sound like they are about as deep as the thinking goes. Deep pain makes you see through them quickly. There are no appropriate clichés about cancer any more than there are shortcuts through suffering. There may be good advice like, "You'll get through this," but you'll have to get through it the hard way—by yourself—before you can believe it. The wisest of my comforters simply left their thoughts at my front door until I could receive them. Then they made their way past me into my living room, willing to sit with me in my pain.

Suffering presses us as humans beyond what we know, so we strain to try to make it make sense. I have certain friends who want to tie my cancer to something I have done in the past. And that event could have been years ago, or even lives ago. Karma? Good grief, I have

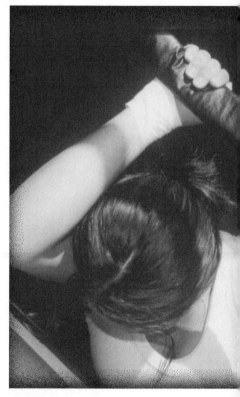

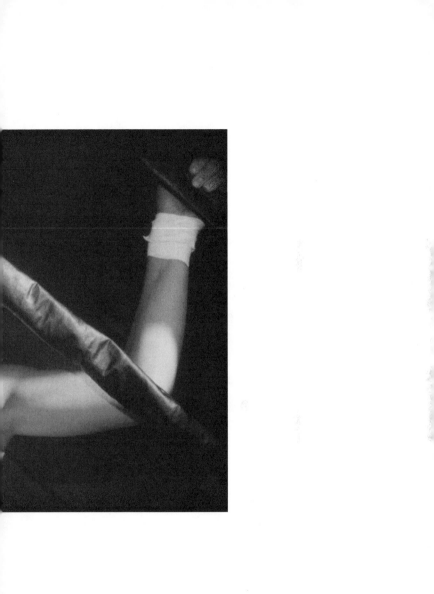

enough trouble keeping up with what I did yesterday. Talk to me about past lives and being chained to the wheel of suffering and I feel about as hopeful as my son's hamster.

Or the phone call from a friend trying to help me accept this beast of cancer by saying, "There's no understanding it now, but somehow it will all make sense in the future." Could be true one day. But thinking you might understand it thirty years from now is little comfort when you're puking your guts up, and you can't believe you'll get through today.

There are also dear friends who think they understand everything now. "This is God's way of slowing you down and making you rest." It sounds like a good theory, and it probably helps them sleep at night. For them, the case is closed; they have solved the mystery of my suffering. But I think, *What loving parent would ever want cancer for a daughter so she could spend more time resting?* That's not the God I've put my trust in.

There is no harder question in all of life than "Why?" I understand the question "Why?" I hear it every day. I'm a mother. I really try to resist answering my kids' questions with, "Because it just is," or, "Because I said so." Their little eyes are pleading and their hearts want to understand. And when I really don't know the answer, I too have been known to make up a reason that will satisfy them. I'm not proud of that. It's selfish. Because the day will come when they learn that the fur on a caterpillar's back isn't there to keep him warm. And while I mean well, I'm not really helping them when I don't stick to the truth, which is, "I don't know." It's such an unsatisfying answer. Yet when it comes to the mystery of suffering, there are countless things we just don't know.

Someone far wiser than I said, "We don't know why, but we know why we trust God, who knows why."

Yep.

ROUND VII

Down, but Not Out

It is maddening to feel as though you are swinging your fists at nothing. I get more tired hitting the air than I would if my blows actually landed somewhere solid. Squaring up with loss is exhausting. I wanted to fight for my breast, but it was already gone. My punches were just swooshes. I was in the ring with emptiness and sadness. In this round there isn't even enough anger left to fuel your energy.

Loss is an inevitable part of living. No one had to tell me that. The problem was my heart stubbornly refusing to cooperate with my head. *You've lost things before,* my head said, remembering specific toys and football games, and that one high school boyfriend. But soaking in the bathtub, gazing down at the mismatch on my chest, my heart says, *No, nothing like this.* It may be just a body, but it is still *my* body.

When you have cancer, you get used to hearing people talk about you in third person. Most of the time I just stand there, happily invisible while they carry on a conversation around me. It's probably easier for others to get the medical facts like a news report from someone else, rather than to directly ask you such personal questions. I overheard one woman I don't even know tell someone else in a whispered tone, "She lost her breast." She was right, except she said it in a way that made it sound as if I'd set it down and forgotten where I'd put it.

The word *lost,* like the word *love,* has been robbed of its deepest meaning because of the casual, inconsistent way we've employed it. We use the word *lost* in regard to direction, or to describe the outcome of a sporting event. We also use "lost" for things we don't really lose at all—like our temper. I know right where mine is. And we use the word triumphantly for things we want to lose, like weight or a few inches around the middle.

There are things that I might call lost, but they weren't really, because I never looked for them, or missed them when they were gone. A button on the inside of my coat, someone's phone number I wasn't going to call anyway—those aren't losses. "Misplaced" is the grown-up word that is better suited for such things. People say, "I've misplaced my glasses." It's temporary, it's small, fairly inconsequential, and most of the time replaceable. No one would ever say, "I misplaced my father at an early age." They would sadly say, "I lost him."

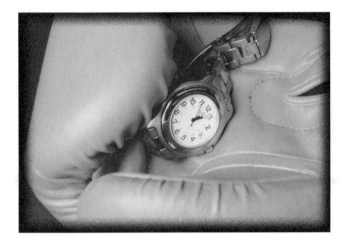

Real loss is not temporary. It's not small or inconsequential; it is up-close and personal and irretrievable. It changes your life forever.

Time is a gentle healer for loss, but healing requires more than time. I will still feel the loss of my breast if I get the wonderful chance to be seventy-five. No, the loss won't change, but my perspective on it will. It already has. You don't think you can live without something until you have to. Cancer is a terrible crucible, but ever refining. How much of my life can I lose because it's made up of tangible things? I want a life made up of things no one can take away. I think about this a lot in the tub as I build up the suds around me. The bubbles help me refuse to let cancer steal any more of life's pleasures.

Suppose I was walking to my car from the

grocery store and a man grabbed my arm and demanded my wallet. After a split second of thought, I would hand over my wallet and even my arm if I could go free with my life. He might not have a gun, but it wouldn't be worth it to me to find out. I'd just give him the wallet. Later, I would have time to think about everything that was in my wallet—my license, my money, my credit cards—and it would make me feel sick to my stomach to think about all I'd lost. The proof of my identity, the value of two hundred dollars cash, my insurance card— the loss of these might seem overwhelming, but not so overwhelming that I would question giving them up.

Now suppose I discovered, in my haste to hand it over, that the inside part had slipped out. Suppose he got my wallet, but he got nothing of what was inside it. That would change everything. Everything of value would still be there. The wallet was nice, but its value came from what was inside.

A breast, or a wallet—I had to give it up to save my life. But the disease didn't get the good stuff. All the me-ness that makes me *me* is still there. The me that laughs too loud at the table, the me that cries at sad movies, the me that believes love changes everything. The cancer thief took my breast, but I have all the value of what was underneath.

ROUND VIII

The Killer Punch

I was in the corner, and no amount of self-talk or cheer-leading was going to get me back into the ring. I had decided I would let the bell ring, and after that, come what may. I would fight this one sitting down, or lying down, if I even had any fight left. I hadn't gotten dressed for a week, and now I didn't even want to get out of bed. *What's the use?* I asked myself. I couldn't even cry anymore. I knew I was slipping, but I didn't know how to hold on.

I was in the ring with an enemy far bigger than cancer. The big "D" is far worse than the big "C." Not death, but Despair. Death can take you only once, but Despair brings death while you live. This dark enemy hides in cancer and divorce and death—in any

overwhelming loss. This enemy seductively whispers in your ear over and over, "You're not going to make it." It's a skunk enemy that sprays its foul-smelling deception at two in the morning, which happens to be the time you're least prepared to fight. "You are totally alone and you're going to die." Lying in the dark unable to sleep, you can almost smell Despair as the weight presses down: "You're not going to live to see your kids grow up and get married."

One afternoon my son walked into my darkened bedroom with his little backpack hanging off one shoulder and announced, "I came to say good-bye." I grabbed him so hard and held on for dear life. I whispered into his hair, "Mommy's not going anywhere, honey. I promise." I could feel the fight for life rising up in me again. And then he said, "I'm leaving to go to Jason's now." And he turned and walked out.

Like osteoporosis of the soul, Despair had silently stolen the nourishment of my hope, robbing me of my last best reason to brush my teeth in the morning. Leaving my soul brittle and hollow, afraid that in living, I might fall and break something. Death before death. Until cancer, I never saw my spirit as something I had to protect. But Despair is crafty. It changes faces and tactics. Like a lioness, stalking you and separating you from the herd, Despair will isolate you from the hope you so desperately need in order to survive. It doesn't matter if you're facing an illness or a bad marriage or the loss of a child—if you don't realize you're up against Despair, it will overtake you, and you'll go down. "Why should I fight anymore? I'm going to die anyway." Well, here's the new press release: *I might die, but not while I am living.*

For the first time in this whole ordeal, I felt gratitude. Cancer can be cut out or treated with radiation or chemo, but bitterness, disappointment, disillusionment, and ultimately Despair are far harder to treat. As someone has said, "The greatest tragedy of life is not death, but what dies inside us while we live."

Some people hear their mother talking in their head, but I hear Winston Churchill in mine: "Never give in! Never, never, never, never!" He was fighting more than a battle, he was in the middle of a full-on war. So when the diagnosis comes, or the attorney has the papers ready, or you're standing over the grave of someone you love, remember—you are still alive. Make it count. You may be forced to die young, but whatever you do, *don't die early.*

ROUND IX

The New Heavyweight Champion

One day, quite by accident, I discovered where angels live and what they wear. They are living incognito as nurses and encouragers in cancer wards. They wear white shoes and try to hide behind kind, radiant smiles. They remind you not to balance your checkbook while you're on pain pills. Believe me, there are easier ways to bring home a paycheck. May God bless the angels who are all around us.

One day one of those angels was reading the Bible to the woman in the next bed. She was in the book of Isaiah, and I heard her say the words "Your hope will not be cut off." I don't know, call my interpretation strange if you want, but that verse rallied me. Yes, my breast, a very important part of me, had been cut

off. But my hope, a far more important part of me, would not be. God was promising that to me right there in my hospital bed. A straight, hard uppercut to the chin of Despair.

A fellow fighter said it better than I could: "Hope is the pilot light that God keeps lit for the flame in your soul." She's right. If the pilot light goes out, there's big trouble. Your initial anger burns out, leaving you cold. Your friends' comfort won't reach you. You actually mail your letter of resignation. You're convinced that God is on vacation. You are in the dark of the long shadow of death. Using the face of cancer, the enemy Despair wins again.

No! I'm coming out swinging. I refuse to put a period in my life where God may have only put a comma. I don't know how long this fight will go on.

I want to beat cancer to live a long life. I want the privilege of growing old and forgetful. I want to sit through boring graduations with tears running down my cheeks. But that is not the real victory in the ring. I could have a lengthy life and not have life at all. The win is mine when the powerful right hook of Hope knocks out the skulking, dark coward called Despair.

Hope is not a positive mental attitude. I have hope but I'm not always positive. There is no way to conquer Despair with happy thoughts. Hope has real strength, but not strength of its own. The power of Hope comes from the truth it hopes in; no matter what the outcome, I can have life, because the loving, merciful God of the universe is good and he is looking after me. So if I fan the flame of Hope every day, I win.

Now I can smile, a lot. Living with real Hope

is like discovering a savings account that was started for me before I was born. It frees me to laugh more and make jokes about things like hair loss and radiation treatment with others who have been there. And to cry my eyes out when I need to. God bless the woman who told me that just because chocolate has no medicinal properties, that does not diminish its healing power. Or the sweet older lady who said, "If you discover a cure for insomnia, call me. I'll be up." I remember noticing as I watched the news coverage on September 11, 2001, there was no time spent trying to resurrect the Twin Towers when they fell. All the energy was spent on saving what might still be alive inside the rubble.

No one who fights with her hope in the Lord ever loses the last round. Today is only one chapter, not the complete book of my life. I have cancer, but cancer

does not have me. Cancer can take my cells, but it cannot take my self. Cancer can have my hair, but it cannot have my heart. Cancer can claim my breast, but it can never claim my spirit!

When the last bell rings, cancer may stand in the center alone, but it will not be the winner. In order for cancer to win, it would have to be able to follow me beyond the grave, and it can't. It will be left alone in the ring with a tired, worn-out shell. My life will be with the One in whom I've put my hope, the Author of everlasting life. He will take my hand in his and raise it in victory.

I praise you because I am fearfully and wonderfully made; your works are wonderful, I know that full well.

— *Psalm 139:14*

"For I know the plans I have for you," declares the LORD, *"plans to prosper you and not to harm you, plans to give you hope and a future."*

— *Jeremiah 29:11*

According to the American Cancer Society Web site (www.cancer.org), the year 2002 will end with an estimated 203,500 reported new cases of breast cancer in women. Studies have shown that *early detection* increases survival rates as well as treatment options. The ACS recommends that women age forty and older have an annual clinical breast exam by a healthcare professional, an annual mammogram, and perform a monthly breast self-examination. Women ages twenty to thirty-nine should have a clinical breast exam every three years and perform a monthly breast self-examination. For more information, consult *www.breastcancerinfo.com.*

About the Author

NICOLE JOHNSON is an actress, writer, and television producer. She is the author of *Fresh Brewed Life* and *Dropping Your Rock*, and is a dramatist with Women of Faith. She makes her home in Santa Monica, California.

A portion of the proceeds from the sale of this book will be donated to a national breast cancer foundation.